Niagara
Falls

Washington,
D.C.

and Prairie,
Texas

New Orleans,
Louisiana

Ross the Reader and the Great Balloon Race

Written by Reid Dailey

Illustrated by Alan F. Stacy

First published by Dog Ear Publishing
4010 W. 86th Street, Ste H - Indianapolis, IN 46268
www.dogearpublishing.net

ISBN: 978-145750-155-5

This book is printed on acid-free paper.

Printed at RR Donnelley
Reynosa, Tamaulipas, Mexico
March 2011

Things had been quiet, a little too quiet, until a masked rider broke the silence of the sleepy little town of Grand Prairie. Miss Ginny Penny was startled by a loud thump on the front step of the town library. Most folks would have been scared but Miss Ginny was excited. She knew it was the Pony Express delivering the Western Gazette. When she opened the paper, she couldn't believe her eyes!

"Jumping jackrabbits, Ross! You've got to read this!"

"Well my goodness! What's all the fuss about, Miss Ginny?"

"Free books, that's what!" cried Ginny.

Miss Ginny handed Ross the newspaper with a headline that read:

Contest to win the world's greatest books!

Ross was a cowboy who loved to read and Miss Ginny was the town librarian. They'd been on many exciting adventures together that almost always involved books.

Ross read on:

> Mr. Melvil Dewey and President Grover Cleveland have announced a contest. Teams are challenged to follow clues that will lead them all around these great United States. The winning team will earn a collection of the world's greatest and rarest books.

"Ross, it's so exciting! We've just got to enter. Melvil Dewey, he's my library hero!"

"Sure as shootin', Miss Ginny! Books and adventure all rolled up into one. That's right up our alley. How about you, Scout? Are ya in?"

An enthusiastic whinny from Scout, Ross's horse, told them he was rarin' to go.

The contest was to be held in just a few days in Washington, D.C. Ross and Ginny read and reread the rules very carefully. They put their heads together to come up with a plan.

"Ross, we just have to bring Grey Eagle with us. He's an expert tracker and we need him for sure. Oh, and of course Miss Ruthie has to come too. The contest says we're going to travel around the United States and she's an amateur cartographer," said Miss Ginny.

"Yes ma'am!" replied Ross. "Her collection of maps even includes some of Lewis and Clark's originals. Gosh! I can hardly wait to hit the trail."

"Another adventure with the gang, how exciting!" exclaimed Ginny.

Soon the big day arrived and the whole town showed up to see the hometown heroes off on their journey. The train depot was packed with well wishers. You have to remember, this wasn't just any old town; this was a town that loved reading and they all recognized that books were treasures!

As the whistle from the steam engine filled the air, Miss Ruthie shouted, "Everyone get on board!"

On the train, Miss Ruthie passed out fried chicken and Bert's Homemade Root Beer from her General Store. They spent the time eating and discussing books. They were thinking about all the sites they wanted to see when they got to the capital.

"I want to see that new monument they just dedicated to General Washington," said Grey Eagle.

"Oh, maybe we could go to the White House and meet the new president, Grover Cleveland," cooed Miss Ruthie. "He's so handsome and smart; I would've voted for him if I could've! I think it's a shame women can't vote."

Washington, D.C. was all abuzz with excitement as they gathered waiting for the contest to begin. Most of the competitors were smiling and friendly, but one team in particular made the mane on the back of Scout's neck stand on end. They were a sinister looking couple with an even more sinister looking horse! They all had equally sinister names: Percival and Prudence Parsimonious and their horse Parsnip. Something told Scout to keep an eye on this bunch, and that's just what he planned to do.

Ross, Ginny and the gang listened as Mr. Dewey and the President explained the official rules. As Ginny gazed in rapt attention at her library hero, Melvil Dewey, the President explained how they would be traveling by hot air balloon across the United States. All of them were distracted by the excitement and the hoopla of the spectacular event. They were lost in their own thoughts.

"Balloons?! Now I'll get to see the eagle's view," thought Grey Eagle.

Miss Ruthie, looking starry-eyed, thought, "I can't believe I'm looking at President Grover Cleveland! He's soooooo handsome!"

"I've read how the heat makes the balloon soar higher; I wonder how you wrestle it in the right direction?" contemplated Ross as he admired the balloons.

Scout was the only member of the gang that noticed the Parsimonious crew was up to no good. He knew it was his duty to help Ross.

Scout couldn't believe his eyes as the Parsimonious rascals wreaked havoc on as many balloons as they could get their hands on. Scout whinnied a warning to Ross as Parsnip chewed through balloon tethers, Prudence ripped sandbags with her hat pin, and Percival set several balloons on fire. But Scout's warning was too little, too late!

Thirty balloons were now fifteen!

If a team wanted to win this contest, they had to nab one of those precious balloons and nab it fast.

With a hoop and a holler, Miss Ruthie grabbed ahold of one of the balloons as it lifted off the ground. Ross, Ginny, Grey Eagle and Scout hurried over just in time to see Miss Ruthie floating away. Grey Eagle jumped for the balloon, but the tether slipped through his hands. Ross, thinking quickly, lassoed Miss Ruthie's ankle and reeled her back to the ground so the rest of the gang could scramble aboard.

Safely aboard the balloon, Miss Ginny unrolled the first clue and read:

In order to win the treasure dear,
Of books and tomes and volumes, 'tis clear.
You must find the home of mists and waters,
Where under the honeymoon rushes four of our five great daughters.

Take a picture of something a horse would wear.
Hint: 551.48

Miss Ginny exclaimed, "Oh, oh, oh, I got it, I got it! In the Dewey Decimal System 551.48 has to do with hydrology. You know, bodies of water, like lakes, rivers and waterfalls."

"Well, 'five great daughters' could be the five great lakes!" replied Grey Eagle.

"Rushin' water, I would map that as a waterfall," explained Miss Ruthie.

Ross chimed in, "I was just readin' in the paper about couples takin' the train up to Niagara Falls for their honeymoon. Do you think that could be the answer to this riddle?"

"Sure do!" they all replied. They put Miss Ruthie's cartography skills to work and headed north to Niagara Falls.

The winds were in their favor. Before they knew it, they had blown across three states. As they approached Niagara Falls, the gang noticed several balloons on an island.

"Perhaps we should land north of those balloons," said Grey Eagle.

"Grey Eagle, I can barely hear you over that loud roar!" hollered Ginny.

"Isn't this excitin'? My parasol is comin' in handy. Where is all of this rain comin' from anyway? There's hardly a cloud in the sky," Miss Ruthie exclaimed.

"Why, that's not rain, Miss Ruthie. That's mist from the falls! Those balloons are on Goat Island! I read about that in a book about Niagara Falls," shouted Ross above the roar.

Pandemonium prevailed down on Goat Island as the dastardly trio struck once again. However, just as no good deed goes unpunished, and every dog (or horse) has his day, Parsnip got his comeuppance. As he sabotaged a balloon, something went terribly wrong. The balloon's tethers snapped, Parsnip panicked, and the basket went spinning out of control over the frigid waters with the horrified horse inside.

"Yikes! That sneaky, low-down critter is in trouble! We may not like it, but we gotta help him," hollered Ross.

"I'll hook that runaway basket with my handy dandy parasol as we fly by!" exclaimed Miss Ruthie.

Quick as a wink, Ross and Grey Eagle jumped down into Parsnip's balloon. Miss Ruthie lost her grip and the basket with the terrified passengers plunged into the turbulent waters. They found themselves tumbling end-over-end in the out of control basket as they dropped like a rock over the raging falls. At that very scary moment Parsnip wished he had been a better horse. Grey Eagle and Ross did all they could to steady the ride.

"Land a Goshen, they're going to drown!" screamed Miss Ruthie.

"Not so fast, Miss Ruthie. I see the basket bobbing in the water. It's a miracle! They're safe!"

The ladies breathed a sigh of relief as they looked for a place to land so they could fish the boys out of the drink.

While looking for a safe spot to land, Miss Ruthie commented, "These falls are purty, but they sure have a peculiar shape."

Scout was familiar with that shape. It looked just like a horseshoe and he knew a thing or two about horseshoes. With a whinny and a wink, he let the ladies know that he had found the answer to the first riddle.

"Thanks for lending a hoof, Scout. Snap the picture quick and let's go rescue the boys!" exclaimed Miss Ruthie.

When they landed, Grey Eagle leapt into the basket and shouted, "Hey look! There's that rotten couple again and they're grabbing all the clues."

In a snit Prudence Parsimonious demanded, "Parsnip, put your equine posterior into this basket, post haste! Those vulgar heathens might have germs!"

As their balloon sailed by, Parsnip leapt back into the Parsimonious' basket, giving Scout a chance to grab one of the few remaining clues.

Fifteen balloons were now eight!

"Quick! We need to find out where we are headed," Ginny said as she unrolled the second clue and read:

The next stop, it's not surprising,

Is not falling but instead is rising.

Our new national treasure is sure to amaze,

Faithfully, every ninety minutes your umbrella you must raise.

Take a picture of a place where our national bird rests.

Hint: 917.3

"Hey, 917," explained Ginny, "is the category for National Parks."

Miss Ruthie was tickled, "Look here, they even have a clue about my parasol."

"You raise your umbrella when it rains. Where does it rain every ninety minutes?" Ginny asked.

Grey Eagle responded, "I heard my brothers in the north talk about a plume of water reaching for the sky many times a day."

"I've read about them. They're called geysers. They're springs that throw a jet o' hot water and steam into the air almost like clockwork," Ross explained.

Miss Ruthie exclaimed, "National parks and geysers could only mean one thing…"

In unison they all yelled, "Yellowstone National Park!"

"Let's get a move on!" Ross hollered. "Miss Ruthie, plot the course with your handy dandy compass!"

But as our heroes headed toward the Territory of Wyoming, the Parsimonious scoundrels were way ahead and nearing the next clue. Prudence asked, "What are those hairy brown beasts down there? I can smell them from here. Let's land near those trees so we can get away from them."

Percival maneuvered the balloon to a large rock clearing. As they were about to touch the ground, they heard a hissing and gurgling sound. Steam and water shot up from the rocks beneath them and knocked them out of their basket. A second burst of steam sent their balloon sputtering off into the night sky. Battered and bruised, they retreated into the shelter of the nearby forest to plot their next move.

As Percival, Prudence, and Parsnip plotted their evil deeds in the shadows, Percival felt someone breathing down his neck. "Prudence, your breath is atrocious."

"That's not me!" Prudence protested.

As Percival turned quickly around, he accidentally knocked a curious grizzly cub flat on its bottom. The cub wailed in protest.

Percival said, "Oh, quit crying you sniveling, smelly beast!"

Big mistake! There's nothing worse than an angry mother unless it is an angry mother bear. At that very moment the moon and stars were blocked out as Mother Bear stood on her hind legs and let out a ferocious roar. "Grrrrrrrr!"

A panicked Percival grabbed a broken tree branch and took a swing at the infuriated bear. His luck must have run out that day because just above his head was hanging the biggest, buzziest beehive he'd ever seen. Honey and bees exploded into the air splattering the three of them. They took off running, followed by angry bees and angry bears. It's funny, but when you're covered in honey, everything you touch sticks to you like glue.

Earlier in the evening, Ross's gang decided to land at the village of Grey Eagle's friends. It was getting dark and it's not safe to go out among the geysers at night. His friends greeted them warmly and threw a powwow in their honor. The night was alive with dancing, drumming and singing.

Grey Eagle explained the contest to his friends and said, "We need to take a picture of a place where our national bird rests."

Ginny said, "Well everybody knows the national bird is the eagle."

"We can show you the eagle's nest at first light," replied Grey Eagle's friend.

They passed the rest of the evening telling spooky stories around the campfire. In the middle of one of the spookiest stories ever, three sticky, gooey, leaf-covered creatures shot straight through the middle of camp.

"What in tarnation was that?"

"It was a monster!"

"No, it was Bigfoot!"

"Whatever it was, it sure smelled sweet as honey!"

Deciding it was a mystery they didn't have time to solve now, they turned in for a restful sleep before the big day that awaited them.

Early the next morning Grey Eagle's friends took them to the clearing. They were amazed by the beauty and power of the geyser. The group then hiked to the eagle's nest. Grey Eagle had always been proud that he was named after the strong and stealthy eagle. They snapped the picture and retrieved the next clue.

But the Parsimonious gang wasn't out of the contest yet. The crooks returned to the clearing where they hijacked another team's balloon.

Eight balloons were now five.

Ready to set sail, Ross and the gang read the next clue.

For the final clue give your horse a rest,
As miles of cable are put to the test.
This new innovation moves people at will,
In a city known for both valley and hill.

Take a picture of a land far away.
Hint: 625

"The 620s are usually transportation," Miss Ginny replied.

"Hey, Scout! You might like this place! I've heard of a new kind of train that pulls iron cars on cables," said Ross.

"I read a story in the newspaper about cable cars being used in San Francisco," added Miss Ruthie.

"Yes, that makes sense. There are lots of valleys and hills in San Francisco," answered Grey Eagle, "but I'm not sure about the land far away. What could that mean?"

Nobody knew!

Miss Ruthie used her map reading skills to chart a course for the final clue. As they flew over the tallest trees they'd ever seen, they observed below them a train huffing and puffing its way westward.

Clang! Clang! Beep! Whoosh! San Francisco seemed to have a life of its own. Their jaws dropped in awe at the hustle and bustle of the hilly city. Landing there was a challenge because of the strong wind, steep streets, and tall buildings.

"How are those cars gettin' up that steep hill?" asked Miss Ruthie. "Where do you think they are headed?"

"Let's climb aboard and find out," Grey Eagle suggested.

"Look at the beautiful clothing those women are wearing," gasped Ginny. "Is that silk? Look at those amazing colors! I'll bet they brought them from their homelands! Ross, that's our clue!"

"You're so smart, Miss Ginny!" Ross shouted above the sound of the cable car.

Miss Ginny approached a young woman in silk and said, "Your clothes are beautiful. Did you buy them here?"

The woman replied, "These were brought from China, but Mr. Wong's Emporium sells them in Chinatown. That's where this cable car is headed now."

In unison the gang exclaimed, "Chinatown! Now that's a land far away!"

As they reached the top of the hill, they saw a burst of color and the excitement of a traditional Chinese parade. They took pictures of the Lion Dance, the fireworks, and the exotic architecture. A festive atmosphere filled the air. Scout was the first to notice that the dastardly Parsimonious trio was stealing film and damaging their competitors' cameras! They were even swiping fireworks. Scout nudged Ross just as Parsnip grabbed their camera with his teeth.

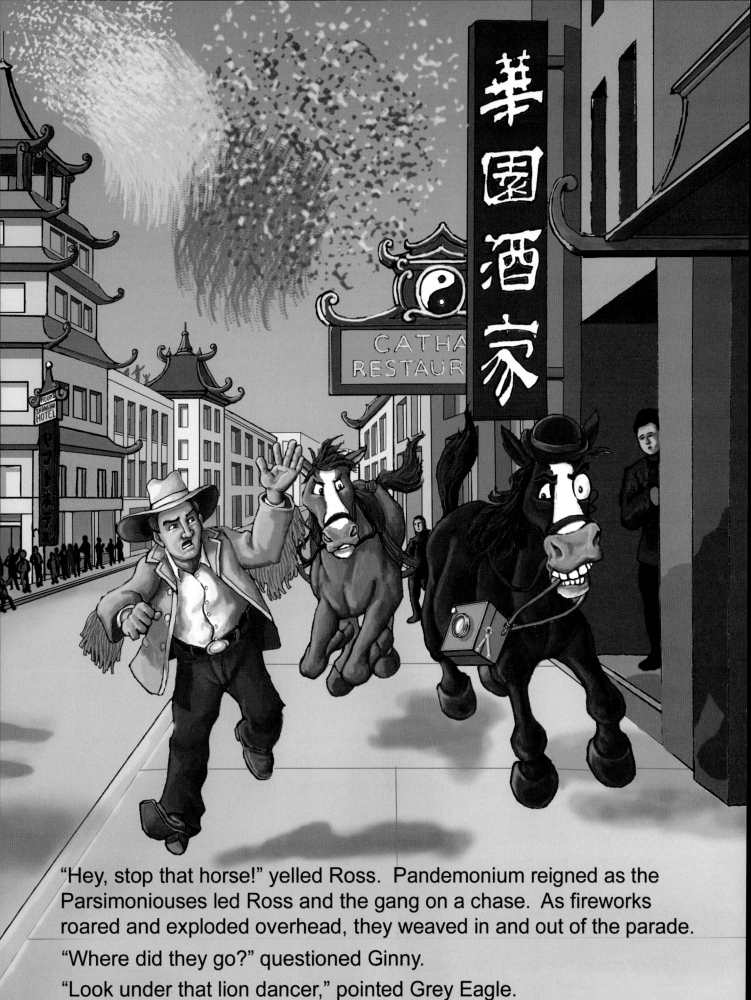

"Hey, stop that horse!" yelled Ross. Pandemonium reigned as the Parsimoniouses led Ross and the gang on a chase. As fireworks roared and exploded overhead, they weaved in and out of the parade.

"Where did they go?" questioned Ginny.

"Look under that lion dancer," pointed Grey Eagle.

Miss Ruthie reached out with the crook of her parasol and snagged their camera just as the villains disappeared like weasels down a hole. A dejected Ross and the gang had no choice but to leave Chinatown and head back to the balloon. They thought all was lost.

"We're in a pickle now! Those rotten Parsimoniouses are way ahead of us. We might as well give up and go home," worried Miss Ruthie.

"It's not over 'til it's over. Fight the good fight. Never ever, ever give up!" urged Ross.

"That's the spirit," Ginny said. "We're not out of this yet!"

While Ross, Ginny and the others boarded the cable car and headed back to their balloon, the Parsimoniouses plotted.

"I know how to slow down that Goody Two-shoes cowboy and his gang!" sneered Percival. "Parsnip, let's ride up beside them and I'll nab that conductor with my cane."

At first, Ross's gang was so deep in thought about their next move they didn't notice their driver was missing. Suddenly the cable car picked up speed and began racing out of control down the steep hill. Passengers started screaming, and mothers on the street rushed to grab their children from harm's way. Ross scrambled to the back of the cable car to pull the lever, causing black smoke to come billowing from the brakes. The crippled car slowed down a bit, but it wasn't enough. Ross took out his lasso and roped a street lamp just like it was a longhorn steer! The cable car came to a sudden stop.

The chaos allowed just enough time for the pesky Parsimoniouses to unfetter all but two balloons. Ross's gang hopped in one balloon while Percival and his pals hopped in the other. The race was on to the finish line in Washington, D.C.!

Five balloons were now two.

Now everything hinged on good navigation and a strong wind. The balloons stayed pretty much neck and neck. The Parsimoniouses started throwing out everything that wasn't tied down to make their balloon lighter for added speed. Ross had to do some expert maneuvering to miss the flying debris.

Washington, D.C. loomed on the horizon as the balloons raced to the finish. The Parsimonious scallywags, in one last effort to win, lit a Roman candle from Chinatown and aimed it at Ross and Ginny's balloon.

Just as the fireball came closer, Miss Ruthie deflected it with a swing of her parasol and exclaimed, "Keep your fireworks to yourselves, you no good scoundrels!"

The fiery missile reversed its course and shot straight through the Parsimonious gang's balloon lighting up the sky like it was the Fourth of July. As Ross and the gang landed their winning balloon safely on the ground, the Parsimonious balloon wasn't so fortunate. It was snagged by the pointed tip of the Washington Monument, and there it hung, dangling dangerously from the tallest and newest building in Washington, D.C.!

The gathering crowd erupted into cheers of delight as Ross, Ginny and the others reached the podium to receive their collection of rare books. The air filled with confetti and the flash of bulbs as President Grover Cleveland and Mr. Melvil Dewey presented the wagonload of books to the contest winners.

Ross and the gang smiled and posed for a picture with Mr. Dewey and President Cleveland. They were pleased as punch as they showered everyone with thanks, loaded up their precious treasure, and headed out for home.

After the lawmen gathered up the villainous Parsimonious crew, they brought them to face the President who sent them to jail.

"Wait!" Ross exclaimed as he handed them a copy of his favorite book, *The 10 Golden Cowboy Rules*. "This might come in handy."

The President scolded them, "Winners never cheat, and cheaters never win!"

The villains hung their heads in shame as they were escorted away.

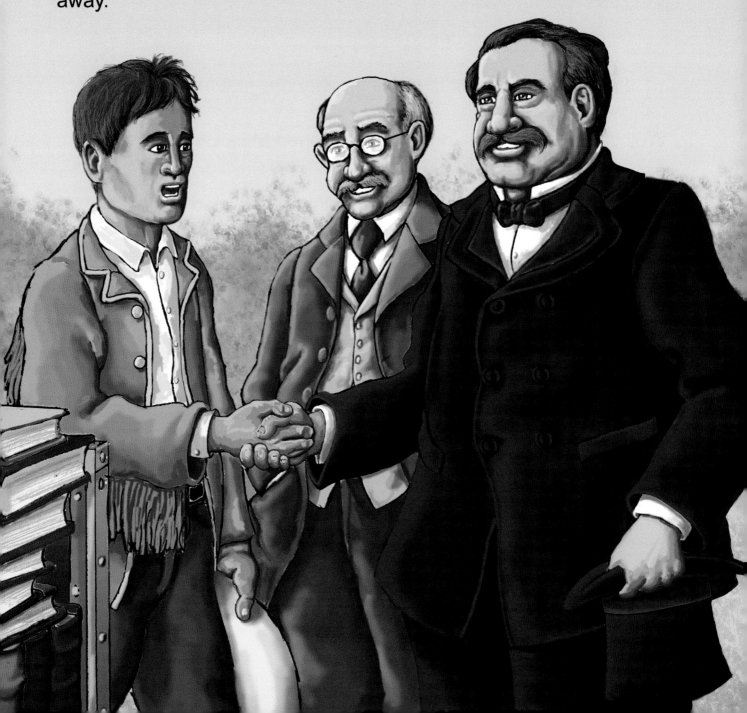

When Ginny, Ross, Scout, Miss Ruthie, and Grey Eagle arrived back home, they were greeted with a hero's welcome. The Pony Express rider handed Ross a letter from Percival Parsimonious. It said:

Dear Ross and the Gang,

We read the book that you gave us about how a good cowboy should behave. We can't make you any promises, but we think we are going to give this "goodness" thing a try. Being rotten doesn't seem to pay! I suppose the best team won!

Less rottenly yours,

Percival Parsimonious

P.S. My favorite rule is reading every day just for the fun of it.

"Well that sure does my heart good!" sighed Miss Ginny.

"Yep!" Ross agreed. "That's my favorite rule too. Sounds like Percival finally got it right! There's a little good buried in all of us; some folks just need a little more help diggin' it out. Come on Miss Ginny, let's go find a good book!"

10 Golden Cowboy Rules:

True cowboys…

1. are honest, faithful and strong.
2. see the good in everyone, even the lowliest scoundrels.
3. rope, ride, brand and read…even poetry.
4. put their fire out before they break camp.
5. keep books in their saddlebag.
6. are kind to every critter, great and small.
7. mind their manners.
8. love their horse, their country, and their mother.
9. always keep their word.
10. read every day just for the fun of it!

Melvil Dewey

Melvil Dewey (1851-1931) was an American librarian who invented the Dewey Decimal System. It is the world's most widely used classification system. Invented in 1876, it organizes all knowledge into ten main classes.

Grover Cleveland

Grover Cleveland (1837-1908) was president of the United States from 1885-1889 and then again from 1893-1897. He was the first president to be married in the White House and the only president to serve two non-consecutive terms. Mr. Cleveland worked to make the government more fair and is remembered for his honesty.

Niagara Falls

Niagara Falls is a waterfall on the Niagara River that lies between Canada and the United States. It was created by glaciers about 10,000 years ago. At peak season as much as 202,000 cubic feet of water flows over the falls per second.

Chinatown

San Francisco's Chinatown is the largest Chinese community outside of Asia and the oldest in North America. It was established in the 1840s and has influenced the history and culture of Chinese immigrants to the United States, as well as being a starting point for many entering the country. It is a major tourist attraction featuring its own government and traditions.

Women's Suffrage

Until 1920, women in the United States did not have the right to vote. The National American Woman Suffrage Association, led by Elizabeth Cady Stanton, worked to change this. In 1920, the nineteenth amendment was passed, granting women the right to vote.

Yellowstone National Park

Yellowstone is America's first national park. Established in 1872, it is located in Wyoming, Montana and Idaho. It is the home to a variety of wildlife such as bison, elk, wolves and grizzly bears. Within the park are hot springs and many geysers, including the most famous, Old Faithful which erupts faithfully every 60   90 minutes.

Ross the Reader and the Great Balloon Race is the third in a series of books written by librarians from the Grand Prairie Independent School District. This collaboration is part of the *Read Across the Prairie* reading initiative started in Grand Prairie in 2005, which emphasizes the benefits of reading for pleasure, free choice of reading materials, and no requirements connected to reading. *Read Across the Prairie* has been recognized at the district, city, and state level, and was awarded the Branding Iron Award and the Wayne Williams Library Project of the Year Award by the Texas Library Association.

Grand Prairie ISD would like to thank the *Ross the Reader and the Great Balloon Race* author committee members: Kathy Brundrett, Monica Dubiski, Belinda Jacks, Kyla Schooling and all the GPISD librarians, for their dedication in creating this book. The GPISD librarians would like to thank Superintendent, Dr. Susan Hull, for her encouragement. They would also like to acknowledge their appreciation to Evelyn Edington and author and performance artist CJ Critt for their guidance and suggestions. A special thank you goes to all past and present Grand Prairie ISD Board of Trustees for their continued support of the *Read Across the Prairie* initiative.

For more information about *Read Across the Prairie* or the first and second books in the series, *The Legend of Ross the Reader* and *Ross the Reader and the Adventure of the Pirate's Treasure*, contact Belinda Jacks, belinda.jacks@gpisd.org, Director of Library Media Services, Grand Prairie Independent School District, Grand Prairie, Texas.